Welcome to

• GENIE STREET •

Join Daisy and Tom on their Genie Street adventures by visiting them at Ladybird's Genie Street website.

Find out about the latest Genie Street books and meet all your favourite Lampland characters!

Written by Richard Dungworth

Illustrated by Sarah Horne

A catalogue record for this book is available from the British Library

Published by Ladybird Books Ltd.
A Penguin Company
Penguin Books Ltd., 80 Strand, London, WC2R 0RL
Penguin Books Australia Ltd., Camberwell, Victoria, Australia
Penguin Group (NZ) 67 Apollo Drive, Rosedale,
Auckland 0632, New Zealand

001
© LADYBIRD BOOKS LTD MMXII

LADYBIRD and the device of a Ladybird are trademarks of Ladybird Books Ltd

ISBN: 978-1-40931-243-7

Printed in Great Britain by Clays Ltd, St Ives plc

Mixed Sources

Product group from well-managed
forests and other controlled sources
www.fsc.org   Cert no. SA-COC-001592
© 1996 Forest Stewardship Council

FSC

THIS LADYBIRD
BOOK BELONGS TO

.........Libary...........

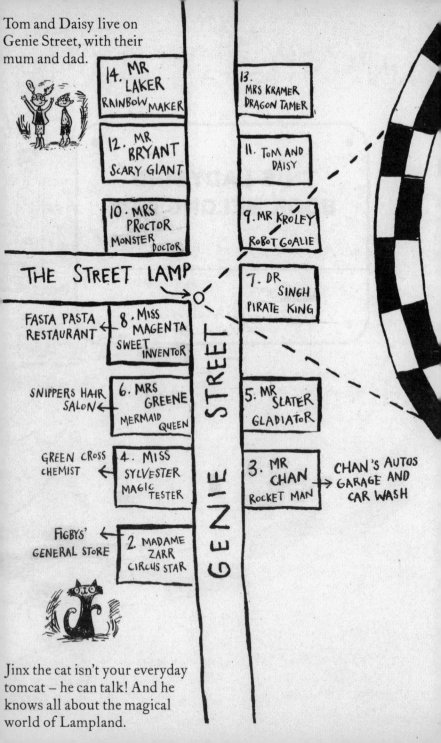

Tom and Daisy live on Genie Street, with their mum and dad.

14. MR LAKER RAINBOW MAKER

13. MRS KRAMER DRAGON TAMER

12. MR BRYANT SCARY GIANT

11. TOM AND DAISY

10. MRS PROCTOR MONSTER DOCTOR

9. MR KROLEY ROBOT GOALIE

THE STREET LAMP

FASTA PASTA RESTAURANT ←

8. MISS MAGENTA SWEET INVENTOR

7. DR SINGH PIRATE KING

SNIPPERS HAIR SALON ←

6. MRS GREENE MERMAID QUEEN

5. MR SLATER GLADIATOR

GREEN CROSS CHEMIST ←

4. MISS SYLVESTER MAGIC TESTER

3. MR CHAN ROCKET MAN

→ CHAN'S AUTOS GARAGE AND CAR WASH

FIGBYS' GENERAL STORE ←

2. MADAME ZARR CIRCUS STAR

GENIE STREET

Jinx the cat isn't your everyday tomcat – he can talk! And he knows all about the magical world of Lampland.

LAMPLAND

to the Noom

Wild Isles

Launch pad

the eventh Sea

Sweet Factory

Rainbow Meadows

Techno Town

City of Ancients

castle Kinghold

to Rossbone Island

Mermaid Reef

Red Dragon Hills

Fairy Forest

Land of the Giants

Monster Mountains

Mr Mistry, Genie Street's postman, gives Tom and Daisy a special parcel which sends them on each new adventure!

Miss Magenta SWEET INVENTOR

Contents

Chapter One
To the Rescue

'Right, I've made up my mind,' Tom told his sister, Daisy. 'I'm having Blueberry Ripple. How about you?'

It was a hot afternoon. The children were on their way to visit the ice-cream counter at Fasta Pasta.

But, as they crossed the road to the shop, Tom's face fell.

'Aww! It's closed,' groaned Tom.

'That's odd,' said Daisy. 'Miss Magenta sometimes pops out at lunchtime, but she should be back by now...'

Miss Magenta was the cook at Fasta Pasta. She made delicious spaghetti. Her home-made ice cream was even better.

'I'm afraid,' purred a voice behind them, 'that she may *never* be back...'

The children spun round.
A black and white cat was
rubbing up against a nearby
lamp post.

'Hi, Jinx!' said Tom.

The talking cat was a friend
of theirs.

'What do you mean, Jinx?'
said Daisy. '*Why* won't Miss
Magenta be back?'

'Because she's being held
prisoner,' purred Jinx. 'In
Lampland. And it's about time
someone tried to rescue her!'

Chapter Two
A Door to Lampland

Jinx rubbed his body against the lamp post again. He began to circle it slowly.

'You're doing the special rub!' cried Daisy. *'Once up… once down… then three times round and round!'*

Jinx winked at her as he completed his second trip round the lamp post.

The street lamp that
Jinx was rubbing was no
ordinary one. It lit the way
to the magical world of
Lampland – if you rubbed
it the right way.

Tom and Daisy had learned
the lamp's secret from Jinx
some time ago. They had
already had several amazing
adventures in Lampland.

Now it looked as if they
were heading there again.

Jinx finished his third circle round the lamp post. The magic street lamp lit up. A ball of light burst from it. Tom and Daisy watched the fizzing purple light-ball zoom towards the door of Fasta Pasta.

As it hit, the 'CLOSED' sign changed to 'OPEN'. The door began to glow purple.

'There!' purred Jinx. 'I think we're all set to go…'

Chapter Three
Parcels and Parachutes

The sound of an aeroplane engine suddenly filled the air. Tom and Daisy looked up.

A little purple plane was looping-the-loop in the clear blue sky. At first, they didn't recognize the person waving from its cockpit. Then –

'Look, Tom!' cried Daisy. 'It's Mr Mistry!'

The Genie Street postman put his plane into a dive – straight towards Tom and Daisy. At the last minute the plane pulled up. Something dropped from its belly. It was a parcel. It floated down to earth, dangling from a tiny parachute.

Tom caught the parcel. He and Daisy read its label.

When they looked up again, the sky was empty.

'When you're *quite* ready,' purred Jinx, 'we do have a prisoner to rescue!'

He strolled over to the door of Fasta Pasta and passed straight through it, like a ghost.

Tom and Daisy looked at each other. Tom tucked the Special Delivery parcel under his arm.

'Here goes!' he grinned.

Together, they followed their furry friend through the glowing door.

Chapter Four
Count Sourtooth

For a few seconds, Tom and
Daisy were lost in thick fog.
Then they stepped out into
a gloomy, grey landscape.
A castle loomed nearby, high
on a cliff top. They could hear
the crash of waves over the
howling wind.

'Welcome to the Wild Isles,'
purred Jinx.

The children stared at the grey-walled castle. It looked *very* spooky.

'Castle Sourtooth,' Jinx told them, over the noise of wind and waves. 'That's where Miss Magenta is locked up. It belongs to Count Sourtooth. He lives there alone – apart from his goblin servants. He's a very nasty character.'

'What has he got against Miss Magenta?' asked Daisy.

'Your friend is rather famous here in Lampland,' explained Jinx, 'for inventing amazing sweets. Her Sweet Dreams factory is legendary.'

'So?' said Tom.

'The count used to be a sweet-maker, too,' Jinx went on. 'But everyone bought Miss Magenta's sweets, not his.'

A sinister laugh came from behind them.

'Not any more, they won't!' snarled a nasty voice.

The voice belonged to a thin, wiry man in a high-collared cape. He was glaring at Tom and Daisy with cold eyes. They didn't need telling who he was.

Count Sourtooth had six goblin guards with him – all with grey skin, ugly faces and sharp-tipped spears.

'What now, Jinx?' whispered Daisy, terrified.

But Jinx had slipped away.

Count Sourtooth approached Tom, scowling. He snatched the Special Delivery parcel. As he read the label, his eyes narrowed.

'So, you are friends of my *famous* guest, are you?' sneered the Count. 'Then perhaps you would like to pay her a visit?' He turned to his goblin guards. 'Take them to the castle,' he barked, 'and lock them in the Tower!'

Chapter Five
The Cat Burglar

Miss Magenta was very pleased to see Tom and Daisy. But getting locked up with her, at the top of Castle Sourtooth's tallest tower, had *not* been part of their rescue plan.

As soon as the goblin guards had left them alone, Tom began searching their cell for a way of escape.

'The door bolts are rock solid,' sighed Tom. 'And the bars over the window are locked in place. Even if we *could* get out of the window, it's a fifty-metre drop to the ground. It's hopeless.'

'Oh, I wouldn't say *completely* hopeless,' purred a familiar voice.

A black and white whiskery face appeared at the window.

'Jinx!' cried Daisy. 'How did *you* get up here?'

Jinx was perched on the window's narrow stone sill.

'It was a *little* tricky,' he purred. 'But my kind make excellent burglars. Allow me to demonstrate…'

There was a padlock on the window bars. Jinx poked one stiff whisker into its keyhole. He twiddled it about a bit. The lock clicked open.

'You picked the lock!' said Daisy. 'Nice going, Jinx!'

Tom still looked glum. 'We're too high up to escape that way, remember?'

'Perhaps *this* might help,' purred Jinx. He pushed something through the open window and jumped down after it. 'Count Sourtooth left it lying around…'

It was the Special Delivery parcel for Miss Magenta.

Chapter Six
Breakout!

Miss Magenta unwrapped
her parcel eagerly.

'It's one of my Sweet Dreams
special selection boxes!' she
cried. 'Just what we need!'

She threw back the box's
lid and grabbed three items
from inside. 'Strawberry laces!
Quickly, unroll them, then tie
them together!'

Tom and Daisy knotted the laces to make one long one. Miss Magenta tied one end to the cell door. She fed the other end out of the window.

'I've invented my own super-stretchy recipe!' she explained. 'It's strong enough to climb down!'

Sure enough, the super-long, super-strong strawberry lace saw them all safely to the foot of the tower.

'Look out!' cried Tom.
Someone had raised the alarm.
Four goblin guards were
rushing their way.

Miss Magenta delved into
her selection box again. She
handed Tom and Daisy a
Sherbet Surprise each.

'Lick the liquorice, then
throw them!'

Tom and Daisy did as
they were told. The Sherbet
Surprises exploded in clouds
of white powder.

The sherbet-coated goblins stumbled into each other. They collapsed in a sticky, tangled heap.

'Ha ha! Gotcha!' whooped Tom. Then his smile faded. More goblins were pouring from the castle. Count Sourtooth was with them.

Tom, Daisy, Jinx and Miss Magenta turned and ran. But there was nowhere to run *to*. Soon they were trapped on the edge of the cliff top.

Chapter Seven
Up, Up and Away!

Count Sourtooth and his goblins slowly closed in. Tom braced himself. Daisy picked up Jinx, ready to protect him.

Miss Magenta hurriedly slipped each of them a block of bright pink gum.

'Chew it, quickly!' she whispered. 'When I give the signal, *blow*!'

Tom, Daisy and Miss Magenta chewed and chewed.

'*Now!*' yelled Miss Magenta.

Daisy blew for all she was worth. A giant gum bubble swelled from her lips. To her great surprise, her feet left the ground. The bubble was lifting her into the air!

Count Sourtooth howled with rage. He leapt forward and clutched at Tom's dangling feet. But the three friends were beyond his reach.

Miss Magenta pinched the neck of her huge gum bubble with the fingers of one hand. She pulled the bubble from her lips, holding it tightly. Tom and Daisy did the same.

'I invented Troublegum specially for airborne escapes!' Miss Magenta yelled at them. 'The bubbles are self-homing! They should carry us back to my factory!'

They drifted high over the sea, until the Wild Isles were out of sight. Their Troublegum bubbles flew in a clear, steady direction, unaffected by the wind.

Tom's arm was beginning to ache when Daisy gave a shout.

'Look! There's the mainland!'

The giant bubbles floated on, carrying them over the cliffs, and on across fields and forests.

Chapter Eight
A Soft Landing

'There it is! Up ahead!' cried Miss Magenta. 'My factory!'

Tom and Daisy peered down at the ground. They were drifting towards a group of brightly coloured buildings.

'When we're over my candyfloss fields, let go!' said Miss Magenta. 'They'll give us a soft landing!'

'Wait for it…' said Miss Magenta. '*Now!*'

Tom and Daisy let go of their Troublegum bubbles. They plummeted into the field of pinky-white candyfloss below. It was like falling into cotton wool.

For several seconds they were lost in a cloud of soft, sweet-smelling fluff. Then, at last, their feet touched the ground and they could see again.

They were back on Genie Street, outside Fasta Pasta.

Tom had the special selection box in his hands.

'But…' Daisy frowned. 'I thought Miss Magenta was carrying that?'

Tom shrugged. 'It's a shame we've eaten them all. But I suppose the box can be a souvenir.'

He lifted the lid. Inside was a whole new layer of Sweet Dreams sweets.

'Wow!' breathed Tom.

The children peered into the box hungrily. Tom took out a Triple-Choc Fizzling Flake.

'Do you know what would go really well with that?' said Daisy, grinning at him. 'A double scoop of Miss Magenta's Blueberry Ripple ice cream!'

She grabbed another flake and hurried through the door of Fasta Pasta, with Tom right behind her.

GENIE STREET

Mr Kroley
ROBOT
GOALIE

Contents

Chapter One
The Impossible Parcel

Tom and Daisy were watching their favourite TV show – *Action Cat*. Mum was working on her laptop. She looked up.

'It's stopped raining, at last!' she said. 'And look – here comes that funny little postman. He's the only one I've ever seen wearing a purple uniform…'

Something landed on the doormat with a thud.

Tom and Daisy were off the sofa like a shot.

'We'll get it!' said Daisy.

Mum had gone to the window. 'Do you know,' she muttered, 'I'm sure he's on a lawnmower…?'

She shook her head and went back to her work.

The parcel on the doormat was much too big to have come through the letterbox. And the front door was locked.

Daisy unlocked and opened the door. She looked outside. There was no sign of Mr Mistry.

'Is it for me?' called Mum.

Tom looked at the parcel's label. 'No. It's for Mr Kroley,' he replied. 'It's come to the wrong house.'

Mr Kroley lived next door, at number 9.

'Shall we pop this parcel round for him, Mum?' asked Daisy. 'We were going to go out and play anyway.' She winked at her brother.

'Okay!' said Mum. 'I'll bet it's more sports kit!'

Mr Kroley was sport mad. He was the PE teacher at Tom and Daisy's school.

Chapter Two
A Lift to Lampland

'What's going on?' Tom asked Daisy, as soon as they were outside. 'I thought Mr Mistry only made a Special Delivery when someone rubbed the magic street lamp!'

Daisy was staring past him.

'I think someone has, Tom!' she said, pointing at the door of their neighbour's house.

Mr Kroley's front door was glowing with purple light.

Tom and Daisy both knew what *that* meant.

The door must have been hit by a beam from the magic street lamp. The lamp stood outside the Genie Street shops. Its purple light showed the way to the magical world of Lampland.

'Jinx must have rubbed the lamp!' said Tom.

Only Tom, Daisy and Jinx, the extraordinary talking cat who prowled Genie Street, shared the street lamp's secret. Only they knew the special way to rub the lamp post to make it work its magic:

Once up…

Once down…

Then three times,

round and round.

Tom and Daisy hurried to
Mr Kroley's door. It suddenly
split in two, from top to
bottom. The door's halves slid
apart to reveal a tiny room.
It had mirrored walls. On one,
there was a panel with a purple
button on it.

'It's a lift!' said Tom. 'Come
on! Let's see where it goes.'

He and Daisy stepped inside.
Tom pressed the button.

Chapter Three
The Big Match

The doors closed and
the lift shot upwards.

'Whoooaaa!' wailed
Tom and Daisy, as their
tummies lurched.

After a few seconds, the
lift began to slow. It stopped.
Its doors slid open and the
children staggered out.

Tom and Daisy found themselves at the edge of a grassy pitch, in a huge, high-tech football stadium. It looked like something from the future. The stands were packed with cheering fans.

'Glad you could make it!' purred a familiar voice.

A black and white cat was sitting on a bench beside the pitch. The cat was wearing a stripy supporter's scarf.

'Hi, Jinx!' said Daisy. 'Where are we?'

'Techno Town football stadium,' replied the cat. 'Merryton United are playing Grotville Rovers. They're old rivals, and Grotville are a dirty lot. It's rough stuff so far!'

There was an angry roar from the crowd as one of the Grotville players made a particularly nasty tackle.

Tom was staring. 'Is it me,' he said, 'or does that player have silver skin?'

'She's a robot,' said Jinx. 'They all are.'

'*What?*' said Tom.

'It's the football of the future here in Lampland,' Jinx explained patiently. 'Real players are far too expensive. Robots are cheaper. Some of them are quite life-like, aren't they? Take Merryton's goalie, for example.'

Chapter Four
Foul Play

Tom and Daisy looked
at Merryton's goalkeeper –
and gasped.

'That's Mr Kroley!'

Their neighbour, it seemed,
was a robotic football star.

The referee gave two blasts
on his whistle. It was half-time.
Mr Kroley came jogging off the
pitch towards them.

As the players came off, a mean-looking Grotville robot shoved one of the Merryton players in the back. He stumbled and crashed into a teammate. There was a loud bang and a puff of smoke. Sparks flew in all directions. Both robots collapsed.

An alarm began to wail.

'Oh, no!' groaned Mr Kroley. He turned very pale. 'They're bringing on the Scrapper!'

A huge machine rumbled out on to the pitch. It scooped up the two damaged robots and dropped them into its awful jaws.

For the next few seconds, horrible grinding and crunching noises came from inside the Scrapper. Then a shower of nuts and bolts poured from its underneath, on to the pitch.

Mr Kroley looked like he was going to faint.

'Are you okay, Mr Kroley?' asked Daisy.

Mr Kroley shook his head miserably. 'We're already losing by four goals, and now we've lost two players!' he said. 'If Merryton don't win this match, we'll be knocked out of the Lampland League! And if *that* happens…'

'What?' said Tom.

'The whole team, including me, will be fed to the Scrapper!' wailed Mr Kroley.

Chapter Five
The Golden Boots

Tom and Daisy were very upset.
They *had* to save Mr Kroley from
the Scrapper. But they couldn't
see how. Then Tom remembered
Mr Mistry's parcel.

Mr Kroley unwrapped it.
It was a purple shoebox, with
two pairs of children's football
boots inside. Tom's face lit up.

'Maybe we *can* help!' he cried.

The boots were made of shiny golden leather. They fitted the children perfectly.

'They make my feet feel all tingly!' said Daisy.

'Mine, too!' said Tom.

The robot players were jogging back on to the pitch. Tom and Daisy quickly tied their laces. They ran out to join the Merryton team – just in time. The whistle blew for the start of the second half.

Tom and Daisy played like superstars. Their golden boots were amazing. The ball did exactly what they wanted it to – however crazy that was!

Tom had the first chance to score. His shot went like a rocket. It swerved one way past one Grotville player, then the other way past another. The ball looped-the-loop and zoomed between the goalkeeper's legs.

GOAL!

Daisy scored next. Her long-range shot sent the crowd wild. She spotted Jinx going bananas.

Before long, Tom got his second goal – with an acrobatic overhead kick.

The Grotville players tried *everything* to get the ball away from Tom and Daisy. But the children just darted past, making the rough, tough robots look very silly.

Daisy celebrated her second amazing goal with a double back somersault. She felt like she could do *anything* in her golden boots.

'That makes the scores level!' Tom yelled to her. 'We need one more goal to win!'

There were only minutes left to play. There was still a chance they could save Mr Kroley.

Chapter Six
Tom on the Spot

Daisy got the ball. She sprinted up the pitch, then hit a brilliant pass to Tom. He ran towards the goal, with just one more player to beat.

The Grotville robot made a wild, desperate tackle. Tom went flying. The referee blew his whistle. Penalty!

Tom put the ball on the penalty spot. He took three steps back. The crowd had fallen silent. Jinx had his paws over his eyes.

'This is it!' thought Tom.

If he scored, Merryton United would win the match. Mr Kroley would be saved from the Scrapper.

Tom took a deep breath. He ran up and swung his golden boot.

The Grotville goalkeeper dived the right way. His metal hands stretched out to block the ball. But at the last moment, it swerved and dodged under them.

GOAL!

The final whistle blew. The match was over.

The Merryton fans went crazy. So did the players. Jinx did a little victory dance.

Chapter Seven
Game Over

Suddenly, the stadium's giant floodlights changed colour. They began to shine with bright purple light. It grew so bright that Tom and Daisy had to screw up their eyes.

The crowd noise faded, as if someone was turning down the volume. The cheering died away to silence.

Tom and Daisy opened their eyes. The children looked at one another.

They were back on Genie Street, outside number 9. They had their ordinary shoes on. Mr Kroley, their ordinary-looking neighbour, was beside them. An ordinary-looking black and white cat was asleep by the ordinary front door.

'Mr Kroley,' said Daisy, 'are you really a robot?'

Mr Kroley laughed. 'A *robot*! Me?'

Then he winked. He lifted his shirt and pressed his belly button. A small panel clicked open in his tummy. There was a metal compartment behind it. Mr Kroley reached inside and took out two shiny medals.

'They're winners' medals,' said Mr Kroley. He hung one round Daisy's neck and the other round Tom's. 'Thank you for saving us. If we ever need players again, I'll be in touch.'

Tom grinned at Daisy. 'We'd better get training then! Fancy a kick-about in the garden?'

Daisy nodded. They said goodbye to Mr Kroley and hurried home, for some more footballing fun!

GENIE STREET

Here's what other children have to say about Genie Street and their favourite Lampland characters!

'This book is really good! I can't wait to read more Genie Street stories.' Callum, age 6

'I like the magical sweets in *Miss Magenta Sweet Inventor*. I wish Troublegum was real!' Milly, age 6

'I really enjoyed *Mr Kroley Robot Goalie*. The children had lots of fun playing football, which was cool as I like football, too.'
Harry, age 5

'I liked the talking cat Jinx. He is my favourite character.'
Amelia, age 5

'I like the way they always have a souvenir at the end of the story to remind them of their adventures.'
Sophia, age 7

Parent note

Genie Street is a brand new fiction series that
is the next step up from Ladybird's Read it yourself
Level 4. Ideal for newly independent Key Stage 1
readers, these books are for children who want
to read real fiction for the first time.

Collect all the titles in the series:

9781409312390

9781409312406

9781409312413

9781409312420

9781409312437

9781409312444

Each book contains two easy-to-read stories
that children will love. The stories include short
chapters, simple vocabulary and a clear layout
that will encourage and build confidence when reading.